M000118184

Mom & Teen:
An Activity Journal and Diary for Mother and Daughter

MOM & TEEN JOURNAL

ISBN: 978-1-7348797-2-8

For more information, visit us
online at www.entrepreneurscolortoo.com

THIS JOURNAL BELONGS TO:

A PICTURE OF BOTH OF YOU
TOGETHER GOES HERE

Suggestions for
Getting Started

This is a journal for both mom and daughter. You can use it to write each other notes. The prompts help guide you with your discussions. You can write about anything you want in the free space, anytime you want. When it's time to read you can put it under the others pillow or in any designated spot you decide.

Mom, imagine if your mom had written you a letter when you were a teen. How much would that have meant to you? I want you to take the lead and write a letter to your daughter...

A letter that she will be able to go back and read one day, as an adult. It could mean the world so let's get started!

Tell her what you like about her and how you feel about your time together.

What are your hopes and dreams for her?

Begin your letter on the next page...

Dear _____,

I want you to always know that I love you. I want you
to know just how much you mean to me.

How well do you know your daughter?

1. Her favorite color is

2. Her favorite sport is

3. Her favorite restaraunt is

4. Her favorite season is

5. What she likes most about herself is

6. If she could choose any pet it would be?

Answers...

1.

2.

3.

4.

5.

6.

MOM

How well do you know your mother?

1. Her favorite color is

2. Her favorite sport is

3. Her favorite restaraunt is

4. Her favorite season is

5. What she likes most about herself is

6. If she could choose any pet it would be?

Answers...

1.

2.

3.

4.

5.

6.

DAUGHTER

FREE SPACE

FREE SPACE

FREE SPACE

FREE SPACE

I'M PROUD OF YOU BECAUSE

MOM

•••••••••••••••••••••   •••••••••••••••••••••

I APPRECIATE YOU BECAUSE

DAUGHTER

TEN THINGS I LOVE ABOUT YOU

● ● ● ● ● ● ● ● ● ● ● ● ● ● ● ● ● ●

1.

2.

3.

4.

5.

6.

7.

8.

9.

10.

MOM

TEN THINGS I LOVE ABOUT YOU

● ● ● ● ● ● ● ● ● ● ● ● ● ● ● ● ●

1.

2.

3.

4.

5.

6.

7.

8.

9.

10.

DAUGHTER

FREE SPACE

FREE SPACE

FREE SPACE

FREE SPACE

COLOR ME

MOM

COLOR ME

DAUGHTER

FREE SPACE

FREE SPACE

FREE SPACE

FREE SPACE

WHAT MAKES YOU HAPPY?

IF YOU COULD DO ANYTHING RIGHT NOW, WHAT WOULD YOU DO?

WHAT STEPS CAN WE TAKE TO ENSURE WE STAY CLOSE AS MOM AND DAUGHTER?

MOM

WHAT MAKES YOU HAPPY?

IF YOU COULD DO ANYTHING RIGHT NOW, WHAT WOULD YOU DO?

WHAT STEPS CAN WE TAKE TO ENSURE WE STAY CLOSE AS MOM AND DAUGHTER?

DAUGHTER

WHAT MAKES
YOU FEEL LOVED?

HOW DO YOU
SHOW PEOPLE
YOU CARE?

WHAT MAKES
YOU CRY?

WHAT BUGS
YOU?

MOM

WHAT MAKES
YOU FEEL LOVED?

HOW DO YOU
SHOW PEOPLE
YOU CARE?

WHAT MAKES
YOU CRY?

WHAT BUGS
YOU?

DAUGHTER

FREE SPACE

FREE SPACE

FREE SPACE

FREE SPACE

USE THIS AS A TEST PAGE FOR EVERY COLORED PENCIL OR CRAYON.

NOW CIRCLE YOUR FAVORITE COLOR

WRITING WITH YOUR FAVORITE COLOR TELL ME HOW OUR
RELATIONSHIP IS DIFFERENT THAN THAT OF OTHER MOMS AND
DAUGHTERS?

MOM

USE THIS AS A TEST PAGE FOR EVERY COLORED PENCIL OR CRAYON.

NOW CIRCLE YOUR FAVORITE COLOR

WRITING WITH YOUR FAVORITE COLOR TELL ME HOW OUR
RELATIONSHIP IS DIFFERENT THAN THAT OF OTHER MOMS AND
DAUGHTERS?

DAUGHTER

WHAT IS ONE OF THE NICEST THINGS SOMEONE HAS DONE FOR YOU?

WHAT IS THE HARDEST THING ABOUT BEING A MOM RIGHT NOW?

I WOULD LIKE TO LEARN HOW TO...

MOM

WHAT IS ONE OF THE NICEST THINGS SOMEONE HAS DONE FOR YOU?

IF A FRIEND ASKS YOU TO KEEP A SECRET THAT YOU DON'T FEEL
COMFORTABLE KEEPING, WHAT WOULD YOU DO?

I WOULD LIKE TO LEARN HOW TO...

DAUGHTER

FREE SPACE

FREE SPACE

FREE SPACE

FREE SPACE

SHARE SOME GOOD THINGS THAT HAPPENED TODAY

MOM

SHARE SOME GOOD THINGS THAT HAPPENED TODAY

DAUGHTER

SPRAY YOUR FAVORITE SMELL HERE

MOM

SPRAY YOUR FAVORITE SMELL HERE

DAUGHTER

FREE SPACE

FREE SPACE

FREE SPACE

FREE SPACE

SHARE A SECRET MESSAGE. NO JUDGEMENT

BUT....

WRITE IT ON A SHEET OF NOTEBOOK PAPER

SHARE IT

CRUMBLE IT UP

THEN TRASH IT HERE AND TAPE IT

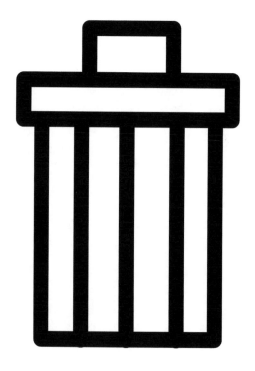

MOM

SHARE A SECRET MESSAGE. NO JUDGEMENT

BUT....

WRITE IT ON A SHEET OF NOTEBOOK PAPER

SHARE IT

CRUMBLE IT UP

THEN TRASH IT HERE AND TAPE IT

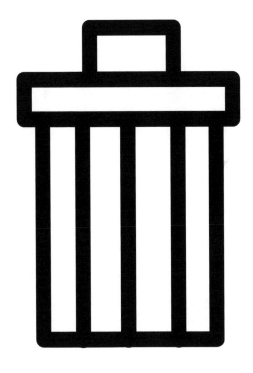

DAUGHTER

WHO IS YOUR BEST FRIEND AND WHAT DO YOU LIKE ABOUT THEM?

WHO DO YOU FIND INSPIRATIONAL?

MOM

WHO IS YOUR BEST FRIEND AND WHAT DO YOU LIKE ABOUT THEM?

WHO DO YOU SEE AS A ROLE MODEL?

DAUGHTER

FREE SPACE

FREE SPACE

FREE SPACE

FREE SPACE

FILL THIS PAGE WITH CIRCLES AND FILL IT WITH ANY MOODS YOU'VE FELT TODAY....LET'S TALK ABOUT IT!

MOM

FILL THIS PAGE WITH CIRCLES AND FILL IT WITH ANY MOODS YOU'VE
FELT TODAY....LET'S TALK ABOUT IT!

DAUGHTER

WHAT I WANTED TO BE WHEN I GREW UP...

_____

_____

_____

_____

_____

_____

_____

WHAT I GREW UP TO BE AND WHY...

_____

_____

_____

_____

_____

_____

_____

MOM

WHAT I WANT TO BE WHEN I GROW UP...

_____
_____
_____
_____
_____
_____
_____

WHAT I ENJOY DOING AS A HOBBY NOW...

_____
_____
_____
_____
_____
_____
_____

DAUGHTER

FREE SPACE

FREE SPACE

FREE SPACE

FREE SPACE

A drawing of my dream car

Where would I drive it to right now?

MOM

A drawing of my dream car

Where would I drive it to right now?

DAUGHTER

THE MOST EMBARRASSING THING THAT HAPPENED TO ME WHEN I WAS IN SCHOOL AND HOW I GOT THROUGH IT

DESCRIBE YOUR PERFECT DAY...

MOM

THE MOST EMBARRASSING THING THAT HAPPENED TO ME AT SCHOOL
AND HOW I GOT THROUGH IT

DESCRIBE YOUR PERFECT DAY...

DAUGHTER

FREE SPACE

FREE SPACE

FREE SPACE

FREE SPACE

MY TOP 5 FAVORITE BOOKS

1.

2.

3.

4.

5.

BOOKS I WANT TO READ

IF YOU WROTE A BOOK WHAT WOULD IT BE ABOUT?

MOM

MY TOP 5 FAVORITE BOOKS

● ●

1.

2.

3.

4.

5.

BOOKS I WANT TO READ

IF YOU WROTE A BOOK WHAT WOULD IT BE ABOUT?

DAUGHTER

·   ·

WRITE A POEM ABOUT BEING A MOM USING THE LETTERS IN THE WORD "MOTHER"

WRITE A POEM ABOUT BEING A DAUGHTER USING THE LETTERS IN THE WORD "DAUGHTER"

DAUGHTER

FREE SPACE

FREE SPACE

FREE SPACE

FREE SPACE

5 OF MY FAVORITE SONGS

CLOSE YOUR EYES AND PICK ONE OF THE 5 AND
THEN PLAY IT FOR DAUGHTER TO HEAR

MOM

5 OF MY FAVORITE SONGS

CLOSE YOUR EYES AND PICK ONE OF THE 5 AND
THEN PLAY IT FOR MOM TO HEAR

DAUGHTER

HAVE YOU EVER LET FEAR STOP YOU FROM DOING SOMETHING?
TELL ME ABOUT IT,

HAVE YOU EVER LET FEAR STOP YOU FROM DOING SOMETHING? TELL ME ABOUT IT,

DAUGHTER

FREE SPACE

FREE SPACE

FREE SPACE

FREE SPACE

WHAT I WISH I COULD SPEND MORE TIME DOING...

HOW DO I HANDLE FEELING OVERWHELMED...

MOM

WHAT I WISH I COULD SPEND MORE TIME DOING...

HOW DO I HANDLE FEELING OVERWHELMED...

DAUGHTER

MY BIGGEST ACHIEVEMENT...

_____

_____

_____

_____

_____

_____

_____

MY BIGGEST REGRET...

_____

_____

_____

_____

_____

_____

_____

MOM

MY BIGGEST ACHIEVEMENT...

MY BIGGEST REGRET...

DAUGHTER

FREE SPACE

FREE SPACE

FREE SPACE

FREE SPACE

DRAW A PICTURE OF YOUR DAUGHTER HERE

DRAW A PICTURE OF YOUR MOM HERE

TELL ME ABOUT YOUR MOM. WHAT WAS SHE LIKE WHEN YOU WERE YOUNG? WHAT DO YOU ADMIRE ABOUT HER NOW?

TALK ABOUT YOUR MOM. WHY IS SHE IMPORTANT TO YOU? IF YOU WEREN'T AFRAID WHAT WOULD YOU ASK HER?

DAUGHTER

FREE SPACE

FREE SPACE

FREE SPACE

FREE SPACE

WHAT ARE SOME FAVORITE PARTS ABOUT BEING A PARENT?

HOW WOULD YOU DESCRIBE OUR RELATIONSHIP?

MOM

WHAT ARE SOME FAVORITE PARTS ABOUT BEING A CHILD?

HOW WOULD YOU DESCRIBE OUR RELATIONSHIP?

DAUGHTER

I REALLY LIKE IT WHEN YOU...

_____

_____

_____

_____

_____

_____

_____

THE MOST IMPORTANT THING YOUR MOTHER TAUGHT YOU...

_____

_____

_____

_____

_____

_____

_____

_____

MOM

I REALLY LIKE IT WHEN YOU...

THE MOST IMPORTANT THING YOU'VE TAUGHT ME......

DAUGHTER

FREE SPACE

FREE SPACE

IF YOU COULD TAKE A TRIP ANYWHERE, WHERE WOULD YOU GO?

MOM

IF YOU COULD TAKE A TRIP ANYWHERE, WHERE WOULD YOU GO?

DAUGHTER

BEFORE I GO TO SLEEP, I SOMETIMES THINK...

I WONDER IF...

MOM

BEFORE I GO TO SLEEP, I SOMETIMES THINK...

I WONDER IF...

DAUGHTER

TODAY I NOTICED...

_____

_____

_____

_____

_____

_____

_____

I AM SO GLAD THAT...

_____

_____

_____

_____

_____

_____

_____

MOM

TODAY I NOTICED...

I AM SO GLAD THAT...

DAUGHTER

FREE SPACE

FREE SPACE

●●●●●●●●●●●●●●●●●●●●●

FREE SPACE

FREE SPACE

I APOLOGIZE FOR...

_____

_____

_____

_____

_____

_____

_____

A SCRIPTURE THAT GIVES ME STRENGTH...

_____

_____

_____

_____

_____

_____

_____

MOM

I APOLOGIZE FOR...

A SCRIPTURE THAT GIVES ME STRENGTH...

DAUGHTER

WHAT 3 WORDS DESCRIBE YOU

● ● ● ● ● ● ● ● ● ● ● ● ● ● ● ● ● ● ●

1.

2.

3.

HOW WOULD YOU SPEND THE DAY IF ALL THE POWER WENT OUT?

MOM

WHAT 3 WORDS DESCRIBE YOU

1.

2.

3.

HOW WOULD YOU SPEND THE DAY IF ALL THE POWER WENT OUT?

DAUGHTER

FREE SPACE

FREE SPACE

FREE SPACE

FREE SPACE

WHAT ARE SOME WAYS WE ARE ALIKE? PHYSICAL TRAITS, PERSONALITY, TALENTS, ETC.

DO YOU KNOW HOW MUCH I LOVE YOU?

MOM

WHAT ARE SOME WAYS WE ARE ALIKE? PHYSICAL TRAITS, PERSONALITY, TALENTS, ETC.

DO YOU KNOW HOW MUCH I LOVE YOU?

DAUGHTER

5 THINGS YOU'RE GRATEFUL FOR...

● ● ● ● ● ● ● ● ● ● ● ● ● ● ● ● ●

1.

2.

3.

4.

5.

5 GOALS YOU HAVE...

1.

2.

3.

4.

5.

MOM

5 THINGS YOU'RE GRATEFUL FOR...

● ● ● ● ● ● ● ● ● ● ● ● ● ● ● ● ● ●

1.

2.

3.

4.

5.

5 GOALS YOU HAVE...

1.

2.

3.

4.

5.

DAUGHTER

FREE SPACE

FREE SPACE

FREE SPACE

FREE SPACE

I ENJOY WHEN WE DO THESE ACTIVITIES TOGETHER...

• •

1.

2.

3.

IF I HAD TO EAT THE SAME THING FOR 2 WEEKS WHAT WOULD IT BE?

WHAT DO YOU THINK I SAID I WOULD EAT?

MOM

I ENJOY WHEN WE DO THESE ACTIVITIES TOGETHER......

1.

2.

3.

IF I HAD TO EAT THE SAME THING FOR 2 WEEKS WHAT WOULD IT BE?

WHAT DO YOU THINK I SAID I WOULD EAT?

DAUGHTER

TELL ME SOMETHING ABOUT YOU THAT YOU THINK I MIGHT NOT KNOW

HOW CAN I HELP OUT MORE AROUND THE HOUSE..

MOM

TELL ME SOMETHING ABOUT YOU THAT YOU THINK I MIGHT NOT KNOW

WHAT WOULD YOU CHANGE IF YOU MADE THE RULES AT HOME?

DAUGHTER

FREE SPACE

FREE SPACE

FREE SPACE

FREE SPACE

Made in the USA
Middletown, DE
18 November 2020